# My Journey Across the Indian Ocean

# Contents

Written by James Adair

Illustrated by Joey Marsh

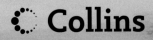

Collins

# The beginning of a crazy idea

I came up with the idea of rowing unsupported across the Indian Ocean when I was living in London with Ben, my best friend from university.

We were both struggling in low-paid jobs, and we read in the newspaper about someone who'd rowed across the Pacific Ocean. It just seemed like an amazing thing to do and although we didn't know where to start, we were excited about it straight away.

When we looked into ocean rowing we found that most people row across the Atlantic Ocean. It's a very popular route and every other year there's a big race organised across it, with about 20 teams taking part. The Pacific Ocean is too big to row as a pair, because you can only take enough food if you're rowing solo, so we started looking at the Indian Ocean.

The route we planned to take went from Australia to Mauritius.

me and Ben

UNITED
KINGDOM

ATLANTIC
OCEAN

PACIFIC
OCEAN

INDIAN
OCEAN

AUSTRALIA

MAURITIUS

The Indian Ocean especially appealed to us because only a few people had successfully crossed it. Eight pairs had attempted it, but only two had got all the way across, and both of those were supported. This means that a support yacht followed them all the time, talking them through how to fix things that broke, or towing them if need be.

One of the reasons so many have tried and failed to cross the Indian Ocean is its length – it's 3,100 **nautical miles** and the Atlantic is only 2,500. Also, during Atlantic Ocean crossings, the currents are always with you because of the Gulf Stream. But the Indian Ocean is very fickle – the currents are everywhere, plus off the coast of Australia there's a big **continental shelf**, so the water is quite shallow for the first couple of hundred kilometres, which makes it very choppy.

When the company that organised the races across the Atlantic Ocean announced a race across the Indian Ocean, Ben and I decided to do it. But as the race got closer we discovered that only two teams had signed up. This meant that there would not be enough money for a support boat. But by this point we were really set on doing it, so we decided to go for it anyway – unsupported.

5

# Starting to dream

Part of my motivation for doing the challenge came from my childhood and becoming seriously ill when I was 14. I developed an illness called Guillain-Barré syndrome, which is a disease of the nervous system. It started a couple of days before I went back to school after the summer holidays. I'd bought some new football boots and was trying to break them in, when I suddenly felt really breathless. The doctor had no idea what was wrong with me, so I went to hospital and within 12 hours of being admitted I was completed paralysed from head to foot – I couldn't see, breathe or speak.

I was conscious but locked in my own body, and spent three weeks in intensive care like that. It was very frightening. The doctors knew I was conscious and that they could speak to me – I could make a clicking sound with my mouth to let them know I could hear what they were saying. So, they talked me through what was going on and said that I'd get better, I just needed to wait for the nerves, which had been destroyed, to grow back. But nerves regrow very slowly – about an inch a month.

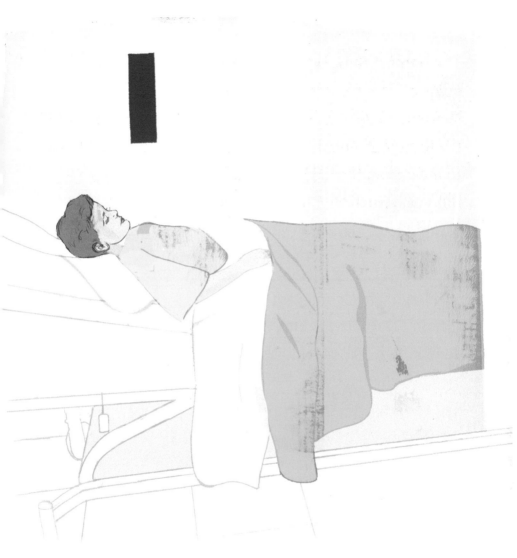

After three weeks I started to see and breathe again,
then over the next three months everything gradually
came back to me from my head down. Well, almost
everything – the nerves didn't quite regrow all the way
and my feet are still paralysed.

The hardest thing was the boredom. Before it happened I was always playing games or reading a book, but suddenly there was nothing to do – I was just alone with my thoughts. People played talking books for me and read to me during the first month before my sight came back. But I was frustrated by how slow my recovery was. I just wanted to get back to school and be normal again.

When I did finally go back to school I was in a wheelchair and couldn't do all the things I'd done before, like playing sport. Instead, I just had to watch from the sidelines. My friends didn't really know what to do or say – it was hard for them to understand, so I learnt to rely on myself.

I remember sitting at the bottom of the stairs in the science block and, because there wasn't a lift or a ramp, going up each step on my bottom, using my arms to push myself up. I became pretty self-sufficient, probably because I was so stubborn and wanted to do everything that everyone else was doing, but my long-term plans did change – they had to.

I'd wanted to go into the army, but that wasn't possible now. So I decided to really live my life and do as much as possible – go on the most exciting travels and take on the hardest challenges.

# Training starts

After coming up with the idea, Ben and I spent six years planning the trip. We had to save up for the boat and prepare ourselves, both physically and mentally. A lot of people told us how tough it would be, so I convinced myself that it was going to be the worst thing ever, so that, if anything, I'd be pleasantly surprised.

Most of the physical training was done in the gym. I cycled to work every day, then I'd do two hours in the gym, or swimming. As important as training was putting on weight, because we knew we were going to lose a lot. But that was the fun bit, just eating mounds of food!

I was working really hard to get into shape, but knew we needed some experience on the water, so we joined a rowing club in London. A member of the club had crossed the Atlantic Ocean, so we talked to him about ocean rowing and he gave us lots of guidance. He told us not to worry about the rowing or fitness aspects, because we would row ourselves fit and rowing is fairly simple. It's much more important to get the boat ready, so we concentrated on that, although we didn't actually practise in it till we got to Australia, four days before we set off.

The boat was second-hand – the cheapest we could find – and had crossed the Atlantic twice, so we knew it had survived some high seas.

It was a good solid boat, made specifically for ocean rowing, just over seven metres long with a watertight cabin at the back to sleep in and a storage cabin at the front. It was quite heavy, which meant that we weren't going to break any speed records, but we knew it was stable in the water.

So most of the work that needed doing was with the equipment – for instance we installed more **solar panels** and built a lot of additional storage.

# On our way

Once we got to Australia, I started to feel really scared.
A man attempting the crossing solo had just set off,
but he gave up after two days. When he got back he said,
"Someone, very soon, is going to die in that ocean."
This was coming from an experienced rower, who'd
already successfully crossed the Atlantic, and we were
due to set off the next morning! I was terrified, but at
the same time excited. I thought as long as we got
beyond the choppy waters of the continental shelf,
we'd stand a chance.

We left at dawn. It was a beautiful morning and the sun was coming up as we rowed out of the tiny marina in western Australia.

It took us about ten minutes to reach the open sea, then it just suddenly went quiet. We had to navigate some of a shipping lane at the beginning, which was quite scary because there were some big ships to get past, but the weather was good and we did about 46 kilometres on the first day.

We could see land for quite a while, as we had to row past a group of islands. This was frustrating, because land signalled that we were still in shallow water and it's safer to be in deeper water where the **swell** is more spread out and there's no on-shore wind. There was a lighthouse we could see at night that kept flashing and it took us four days to lose sight of that completely.

When we got to the furthest island, we really felt like we'd made it. It had been tough – because of the currents we'd been rowing hard but only making slow progress. Finally we were heading out into the expanse of ocean and really on our way.

It was a beautiful, sunny day, so we thought we'd celebrate with our first swim, but at that moment a massive great white shark **breached** to take a sea bird that was sitting on the water about 50 metres from us. It was close enough to see the rows of teeth, so, funnily enough, we didn't go for a swim. Not then and not for another week!

# Life at sea

We probably tried every possible different pattern
of rowing. We certainly had enough time to, but we
settled on two hours on, two hours off during the day,
three hours on, three hours off at night. It's really tricky to
get in and out of the cabin when it's dark, so that's why
it was slightly longer at night.

We made a point of eating at the same time at the beginning, because we thought it was important to spend a bit of time together – if you're taking it in turns to row and sleep you don't actually spend any time together! So for the first two months one of us would cook, we'd stop and eat together, than start rowing again.

However, we eventually noticed that if we weren't rowing for, say, half an hour during each meal, we were in fact losing an hour and a half each day. So we ended up taking it in turns to eat as well.

The food was divided into day packs, each pack containing four freeze-dried meals – breakfast, lunch, dinner and pudding. Then we had a chocolate bar and a snack pack which was either nuts or sweets. We also had vitamin supplements, cups of soup and honey.
It wasn't very appetising at the beginning, but when after about two weeks of rowing we became really, really hungry, it was the best thing ever!

At first, the meals had filled us up, but as we began to lose weight we just became hungrier and hungrier.
It got to the point when all we could think about was our next meal and we were never full. Our regular breakfast was to melt a chocolate bar into our porridge, then pour on honey and add extra raisins – that was about 1,200 calories, but we were still hungry.

The bed was a mattress in the cabin and it was very comfortable. We had a cotton sleeping bag each and a rug.

It was very cold out on the ocean and we ended up wearing our foul weather gear all the time because we were constantly being smashed by waves, swell, wind and rain. When the weather was really rough we had to tie ourselves to the boat, so as to avoid being washed overboard. But when the big waves hit, we did lose things.

On day 75 we had a bad experience with a wave. I was coming out of the cabin, so the door was open, when a massive wave hit us side on. Ben had stopped rowing and was taking down our daily position, so we were caught unawares and the whole boat filled up with water, including the cabin. Everything was soaked and we lost a lot of things, such as the digital compass, batteries and cushions from the seats. Even worse, the electrics were ruined, which meant no **global positioning system** (GPS) for navigation and no cabin lights.

We suddenly went from being on a boat that had felt quite hi-tech to something very basic. We now just had a hand-held GPS that we only turned on every six hours to save the batteries, and we were only halfway across!

Everything in the cabin had got wet and I remember lying in what was basically a big puddle, knowing we were in a bad situation because everything had got wet or been broken. It was pitch black and I couldn't get to sleep – it was awful.

The mattress stayed wet for three days and nights before it was sunny enough to dry out.

Losing the fancy GPS hit Ben really hard – he'd always been more into working out distances than me, and when it broke he was very frustrated. I was quite pleased that I didn't have to spend my time rowing and staring at the GPS trying to work out if we were pointing in the right direction, how fast we were going, or how much distance we were going to cover over the next three hours.

Now, there was nothing to look at apart from the compass and, at night, the stars. With the cabin lights no longer working, we could see the stars really clearly and we did everything at night by starlight. The **Milky Way** arched brightly over us, shooting stars flared across the sky and the water glowed with the **bioluminescence** of **plankton**. When we put the oars in, the plankton would light up and suddenly the sea would go green and gold. We were out in the middle of a weird, wonderful, beautiful world.

However, because we were only turning the manual GPS on now and again, sometimes we'd find that we'd just been going around and around in circles for hours. We'd thought we'd been going really fast, but had actually just been trapped in huge whirlpools and not going anywhere!

25

# All-time lows

Soon after the day-75 wave, I got very bad salt sores caused by a build-up of salt on my skin due to the lack of fresh water. They're incredibly painful.

We also developed "claw hand" – because we were holding the oars all day, we couldn't straighten out our fingers. In fact, way back at the beginning on about the third day we were trying to fix something on the boat and Ben was holding the most important tool on the boat and I was holding the second most important one, when my claw hand got the better of me and it seized and I dropped the tool into the water. Ben saw it falling and tried to grab it, but in doing so he dropped his tool. We just had to sit there and watch these two perfect tools disappear into the blue. Actually after that we just burst out laughing, because it was so bad it was funny.

Most of the kit on the boat broke at some stage.
The freshwater-maker broke on day seven, which was
a disaster, because then we had to use the hand-pump,
which meant we had no free time. After sleeping for eight
hours a day and rowing for 12 in total, we were left with
four hours' free time. But when the water-maker broke we
had to hand-pump for two hours each day. It was really
tough because we were so tired and the extra pumping on
top of the rowing was a bit depressing at the beginning,
but we turned it into a positive and used the time to talk.
We also read *Moby-Dick*, the famous book about
a sailor hunting a whale, aloud to each other,
which was quite fun.

For me though, the hardest thing was getting up in
the middle of the night to row. Getting out of the cabin
was difficult in itself because at night you couldn't see
much and if you could hear rain coming down and waves
washing over, it felt impossible. But my motivation to
prove that I could do it kept me going, plus I'd signed up
for a great adventure and we always knew we'd have to
overcome many difficulties on the way.

# Sharks, squid and flying fish

We saw loads of amazing things too – the wildlife was definitely a highlight for me. At one point a shark scraped up against the side of the boat and a two-metre blue shark circled us for a couple of hours too, which felt exciting rather than scary at the time. Sometimes we'd just see a fin, which somehow felt more threatening, so we tried not to think too much about what was out there.

We saw fin-backed whales and pods of whales. We'd be rowing and suddenly they'd be there, but they'd be gone again quite quickly. At night we could hear them spouting, slapping their tails and calling.

We were visited by a massive pod of pilot whales one day. At first, we could hear their sonar clicking all around us really loudly. It actually woke Ben up – he thought the GPS had started working again! Then suddenly they were there, all around the boat. One was sitting up on its tail, just looking at us. It was a bit nerve-wracking, because they're pretty big, but it was also really amazing to be so close to them. We'd been at sea for so long that it felt like it had become our world, but this reminded us that it was their world too and we were just passing on our different journeys.

We had dorados following us every day. They're big, green, blunt-nosed fish, called dolphin fish sometimes because they play like dolphins. They're beautiful, a really stunning colour and are often in pairs. They'd jump around the boat, obviously showing off to each other and surfing in the waves behind us.

We also saw shearwater birds every day. They never flap their wings, simply use the thermals to glide really low to the ocean.

There were also tiny storm petrels, which are small sea birds that appear in storms. In really massive seas these little birds would appear almost to run over the water, dipping their beaks in to catch plankton.

There were flying fish, too, and I nearly got hit in the face by one. But the all-time highlight, and the weirdest and most amazing experience of my life probably, was giant squid. One night there were no stars at all, just thick clouds and a heavy atmosphere. I was rowing away and all I could see was the occasional bioluminescence from the plankton, but suddenly there was a huge milky white, rolling mass underneath the boat. It was a giant squid. I got Ben up and we sat there watching it – it was the most incredible thing I've ever seen, like an alien, but as big as a car, just rising and falling below the surface. We saw it two nights in a row, then never again.

# The home straight

We had some very bad weather coming towards Mauritius.
There were 35 knots of wind, rain and strong currents
pushing us south when we were trying to get up to
the north of the island, past some reefs along
the east coast. We tried rowing together for extra power,
but we still couldn't do it. We spoke to our weather router,
who said there was a very small gap in the reef that we
should aim for.

He gave us the co-ordinates to head for and said he'd
come out to meet us on a boat and escort us in. So, we
turned around and sped towards the gap in the reef.
It was about 24 kilometres away, but because the wind
was now behind us we were blown very quickly towards it.

We thought we'd be at land by 5 o'clock that afternoon,
so we ate our last potato and leek soup. Before long,
we could see the high volcanic peaks of Mauritius –
it was so exciting. Our main aim was to reach the reef
entrance before nightfall because we knew it would be
quite tight to get through, so it was best not to try doing it
in the dark.

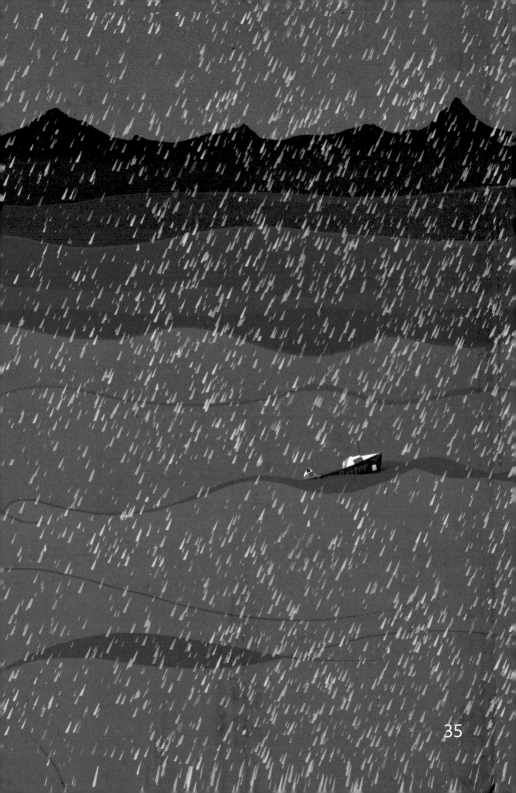

We saw the lighthouse that the weather router had told us to look out for and headed for that, expecting to see him coming to meet us. However, the waves inland were getting bigger, and as we got closer to them we started to feel more and more nervous.

Despite this, we were still excited, as we thought we were coming into a celebratory arrival, so we cleaned our teeth and put on our best foul weather gear. We thought we should make a bit of an effort as we were about to return to civilisation.

# Disaster again

I'd stopped rowing to stand up and try to spot the rescue
boat, when a huge wave appeared from nowhere.
We hadn't been hit by any other waves on the way in,
but suddenly this massive wave – six metres of white
rolling water – was coming towards us, three times as
tall as us.

We were able to see it for a full five or six seconds before it hit us. I just looked at Ben and he shook his head – we knew immediately that it was going to **capsize** us.
I really thought it would kill us.

The last thing I remember seeing was Ben holding on to the sides of the boat, then I took a really deep breath and bang, the wave hit us.

It just demolished us. Everything went black and I came up about two and a half metres away from the boat. The boat self-righted, but everything was destroyed. The cabin was ripped out, the oars were snapped, the rowing seats were torn away and the radio antenna was broken.

Everything was in the water, including our video camera with two months of footage of the voyage. The **flares**, which we'd planned to light as we arrived, were scattered around us, sinking.

We clambered back on to the boat, but there was no time to feel relieved that we were both still alive. How were we going to control the boat without any oars?

Then I had an idea. I jumped back into the water to rescue the flares. We knew a boat was coming to find us, so I thought we could set off the flares to help them locate us.

As I set off a flare, the discharge cut my finger
quite deeply. I turned around to warn Ben to be careful,
but he was already firing another flare. The discharge
from it flew into my leg, cutting me to the bone. It was
a hole about the size of a ten pence piece and blood
started gushing out of it. But before we could think about
how to stop the bleeding and the pain, I saw another wall
of white water coming towards us.

We thought this wave would probably capsize us again, so I suggested we jump in the water and hold on to the boat from there – I thought it would be safer.

I realise now it was a ridiculous thing to do because the power of the wave picked the boat up and flung it far away. So, the boat was gone and suddenly we were treading water in the sea, with no boat and no lifejackets – nothing apart from what we were wearing. Immediately I took my clothes off because they were quite heavy, then we saw the boat that had come to rescue us. It was further out to sea, so there was nothing for it but to start swimming towards it – away from land.

The giant waves were now coming in on a regular basis. Each time, we'd duck underwater, holding on to each other so we didn't get separated, then we'd come back up a few seconds after the wave had passed. All the while, Ben was looking underwater for sharks, because we both knew that the blood from my leg could attract them.

Every so often we'd see the rescue boat in-between the waves, then suddenly it was gone. Later, we found out the people on board had seen our boat being flung into shore, but they hadn't seen us in the water. Because of the **cyclonic** conditions, they'd had to turn around and go back to shore. It was now getting dark, which we knew would be a particularly dangerous time for sharks – someone had been killed by a shark in this exact stretch of water. We had to try to do something to save ourselves. We couldn't just tread water, in the dark with no lifejackets and huge waves breaking over us.

So we decided to swim towards the lighthouse and the gap in the reef. We could only hope we would find it in the dark.

We got closer and closer to the reef, then suddenly we were standing. The next wave washed us fully on to it. We hoped we were getting closer to safety, but found we'd also been cut all over our bodies by the sharp **coral**.

We tried to crawl our way over the breaking waves, but it was very painful because we kept falling over on to more bits of coral and our feet were soon cut to shreds. So we sat down in the water and tried to calm down.

We checked ourselves over. We realised our cuts weren't too bad, just painful, so we tried to feel positive. After all, we could see land, the moon was high in the sky by now and we had good visibility. We decided to wait for a bit, then discuss our options.

One of our plans was to wait for the tide to come up, then swim in over the coral. But the danger was that the tide would bring the breaking waves closer and we might be swept away by the strong currents. Also, swimming three kilometres when we'd only had one packet of soup each all day felt impossible. We'd rowed all day solidly, capsized, swum for an hour, I was bleeding, we were exhausted, in shock and it was getting cold as well, so I just wasn't sure we had it in us. Then a helicopter suddenly appeared.

That was it, brilliant, the helicopter would see us and we'd be saved. The helicopter did quite a few loops, but kept missing us, just. We were shouting, whistling and waving our hands to try to attract its attention. Eventually its searchlight illuminated us totally and we thought we were saved, but then it circled away and hung over the likely position of our boat for a minute.

The helicopter finally went low before disappearing over a hill. Everything was silent again. That was tough – we had to accept that we might be out on the reef all night.

# Two French Mauritians and a mattress

The wind had picked up and we were shivering. We were wearing just thin clothes and **hypothermia** was starting to set in. After about half an hour we saw another sweeping light. We immediately started whistling and shouting together until the light came to rest on us. It was from a boat that had come to look for us.

Voices called out to acknowledge us and ten minutes later we saw two guys walking over the reef towards us. We later found out they were called Thierry and Eric. They were local men who'd just been watching television, when someone had phoned them to say that a couple of English guys had gone missing on the reef and they came out to look for us.

They went back to their boat to fetch some mattresses. We lay on these while they floated us over the coral and back to their boat. We were enormously grateful to them for coming to our rescue, though I think it was quite exciting for them too, to find and save us.

I just had eyes for my family because I'd missed them so much. So, as soon as I got off the boat I tried to walk towards them, but I was weaving all over the place because I hadn't walked for 116 days. My leg muscles had become wasted and I was land-sick because I was so used to the movement of the boat. But it was the best feeling in the world to see my family again.

Ben's family and mine had been on Mauritius for about two days, getting more and more worried because of the storms. That night it was pitch black, the wind was howling and our boat had been found without us in it, so they feared the worst and thought we were lost at sea. It was a huge relief to all be together again and everyone was hugging.

# Back to normality, sort of

After a bit of a holiday and some stitches in my leg,
we came back to London and life got back to normal,
more or less. I decided not to go back to my old job.
I'd had a lot of time to think out there on the rowing boat
and had decided to try something that I really wanted to
do – become a writer.

I'd also like to do another sea challenge, but not rowing
– perhaps on a sailing boat or a motor boat of some sort.
And I'd like to travel more, so yes, there will be
more adventures!

# Glossary

| | |
|---|---|
| **bioluminescence** | light given off by some living animals |
| **breached** | made a gap and broke through it |
| **capsize** | turn upside-down in rough seas |
| **continental shelf** | shallow seabed around a continent |
| **coral** | a hard rock-like substance made from the skeletons of tiny sea creatures |
| **cyclonic** | related to cyclones, powerful tropical storms with strong winds and heavy rain |
| **flares** | handheld rockets that produce a bright flame |
| **global positioning system** | a navigation system that uses information from satellites |
| **hypothermia** | a dangerously low body temperature |
| **Milky Way** | the galaxy of stars that contains the Earth |
| **nautical miles** | units used to measure distance at sea; one nautical mile = 1,852 metres |
| **plankton** | microscopic creatures that drift in water |
| **solar panels** | panels that absorb the sun's rays and turn it into electricity |
| **swell** | rolls of waves that happen out at sea |

# Index

# The adventure of a lifetime

Rescued!

MAURITIUS

Day 116

see a pod of
pilot whales

Capsized!

wave fills boat
with water

see a
giant squid

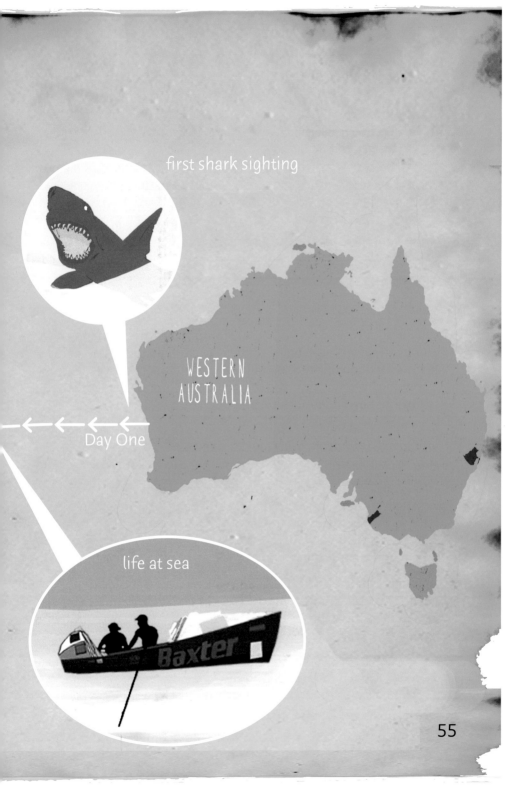

first shark sighting

WESTERN
AUSTRALIA

Day One

life at sea

Baxter

# Ideas for reading

Written by Clare Dowdall BA(Ed), MA(Ed)
*Lecturer and Primary Literacy Consultant*

**Learning objectives:** understand underlying themes, causes and points of view; compare how writers present experiences and use language; use the techniques of dialogic talk to explore ideas, topics or issues

**Curriculum links:** Geography; P.E.

**Interest words:** bioluminescence, breached, capsize, continental shelf, coral, cyclonic, flares, hypothermia, nautical, plankton, solar panels, susceptible, swell

**Resources:** paper and pens

## Getting started

*This book can be read over two or more reading sessions.*

- Explain that this book is an autobiography. Discuss what an autobiography is, and how it differs from a biography. Revise the features that are likely to be found in an autobiography, e.g. it recounts a life story, it is written mainly in chronological order, in the first person, it may use colloquial terms.

- Ask children to read the blurb in pairs. Discuss what the word *unsupported* means in this context, and share any experiences of rowing or any famous rowing events that the children know about.

- Turn to pp2–3 and locate the Indian Ocean on the world map. Based on this, discuss what other challenges Ben and James might have faced, e.g. the heat, the length of the journey, hunger, fatigue.

## Reading and responding

- Ask children to read pp2–5. Discuss why they think the Indian Ocean is harder to row across than the Atlantic Ocean. Support and encourage inferential reading through questioning, e.g. *Why didn't the Atlantic Ocean appeal to Ben and James? What does this tell you about their personalities?*

- Ask children to read pp6–9 about James's early life, silently. Ask children to focus on James's statement: *So I decided to really live my life and do as much as possible.* Using this statement, discuss how James is presenting his story, and what his perspective on his illness is.

- Ask children to read to the end of the autobiography, noting high and low points in Ben and James's journey.